Gary the Goose Belonged

Stephen and Karen Rusiniak

Illustrated by Donna Rusiniak

Gary the Goose Belonged by Stephen and Karen Rusiniak

Published by Pen It! Publications, LLC in the U.S.A.

812-371-4128 www.penitpublications.com

ISBN: 978-1-63984-242-1

Illustrated by Donna Rusiniak

Gary the Goose belonged, just as he should.
He was everybody’s friend and a proud member
of the flock.

But late one autumn afternoon, and during the flock's flight south for the winter, something happened that would change Gary’s world forever.

Gary and Gwendolyn would eventually make a nest together and the following spring...

...when the eggs hatched,

six new goslings joined their family.

Arriving at the pond,

most of the flock landed in the water,

but not Gary.

He landed on the hard, grassy ground,

and when he did,

he injured his leg, badly.

The other geese swam ashore to where Gary was and began feeding on the grass. But not Gary.

When it was dark and while the geese rested. Gary tried to make his leg feel better.

He finally fell asleep just as the sun was rising, and moments before the other geese were preparing to leave.

They saw Gary sleeping but they didn't wake him or tell him that it was time to go because while he looked mostly like them, his leg didn't and *that* made him different.

The flock flew away without even saying goodbye!

Several days passed before Gary could walk.
His hurt leg had slowly healed,
but forever more
it would remain slightly twisted,
unlike his other leg
and unlike the legs of the other geese
that arrived on the pond every afternoon.

Gary was always there
to greet them when they landed,
but once they had all left the water,
and walked on the grass,
they saw his leg and turned away, after all,
Gary's leg looked different from theirs.
Try as he would,
Gary couldn't make friends...

...that is, until he did.

Doris the duck,

who was raising three darling ducklings

all by herself

arrived one morning,

and she and the ducklings

liked the pond so much that

they decided to stay for a while.

Gary introduced himself to the pond's newest residents, and much to his surprise...

...they didn't care about his leg or how he looked.

They simply accepted him for who he was.

Gary and Doris,
and the darling ducklings
decided to make it their job
to greet each new flock of geese
as they arrived every afternoon...

...and then to wish them well

the following morning when they left.

Gary was happy again because of his new duck friends, but something was about to happen that would change his life forever.

One afternoon,

as another gaggle of geese was landing...

...Gary and Doris and the darling ducklings swam to the middle of the pond to greet them.

Swimming back to shore, Gary looked just the same as the other geese until they all reached the grass.

The other geese quickly noticed his twisted leg and how it looked as he struggled to walk from the water.

Once again, Gary was seen as being different, and that was that. Except it wasn't.

Gwendolyn the Goose was watching

as Gary struggled to leave the water.

Rather than turning away, Gwendolyn went to Gary

and gently nudged him up onto the grass.

Gary had made a new friend.

As the other geese began feeding, Gwendolyn stayed by Gary, all afternoon, and then all night too.

In the morning, as the flock was leaving, Gwendolyn decided to stay.

She wished the flock well on their journey, as she waved goodbye beside Gary and Doris and the darling ducklings.

Later that same spring, Doris and the darling ducklings said goodbye to the pond,

and left for their real home up north.

Gary and Gwendolyn, however, would continue living on the pond for the rest of their lives.

They became teachers...

...who taught each newly arriving flock that who you are inside is so much more important than how you appear on the outside,

and that being different doesn't mean that you can't fit in, it doesn't mean that you can't belong.

Gary the Goose belonged, just as he should, and just as he always would.

Let's talk...

1. If Gary came to visit your class, what do you think he would talk about?

2. Why do you think Doris and her darling ducklings became friends with Gary?

3. When he was struggling to get out of the pond why did Gwendolyn decide to help Gary?

4. If you could continue Gary and Gwendolyn's story, what would you want it to say?

Stephen Rusiniak is a retired police detective who specialized in juvenile/family matters. Today he shares his thoughts through his writing, which includes stories that have appeared in various magazines, newspapers, and several books in the *Chicken Soup for the Soul* series.

As a former special education teacher, Karen Rusiniak has seen firsthand how difficult it was for special needs children to fit in with their peers as well as their struggles to make friends.

Karen never gave much thought to writing. “Me writing a book. No. Steve is the writer in the family.” But, when Steve, her husband, asked her to help him with an idea for a children’s story, she jumped right in. “Being a part of this writing process has been an extremely rewarding and totally new experience,” she has since discovered.

And when Steve and Karen needed an illustrator for their new story, they knew just who they wanted: another family member, Steve’s sister-in-law, a retired art teacher, Donna Rusiniak. An accomplished artist, Donna has had her work displayed in galleries in her home state of New Jersey, in New York, and in Key West, Florida.

Stephen and Karen reside in Wayne, NJ, and West Ocean City, MD. Donna resides with her husband, Paul, in Wayne, NJ.

Made in the USA
Middletown, DE
13 November 2022